Ruff Day

Sigmund Brouwer

illustrated by
Sabrina Gendron

orca Echoes

ORCA BOOK PUBLISHERS

For Jenna and Lauren and Dees.

Text copyright © Sigmund Brouwer 2021
Illustrations copyright © Sabrina Gendron 2021

Published in Canada and the United States in 2021 by Orca Book Publishers.
orcabook.com

Library and Archives Canada Cataloguing in Publication
Title: Ruff day / Sigmund Brouwer ; illustrated by Sabrina Gendron.
Names: Brouwer, Sigmund, 1959- author. | Gendron, Sabrina, illustrator.
Series: Orca echoes.
Description: Series statement: Orca echoes | Charlie's rules ; #2
Identifiers: Canadiana (print) 20210095075 | Canadiana (ebook) 20210095083 |
ISBN 9781459825895 (softcover) | ISBN 9781459822641 (PDF) |
ISBN 9781459822658 (EPUB)
Subjects: LCGFT: Novels.
Classification: LCC PS8553.R68467 R84 2021 | DDC jc813/.54—dc23

Library of Congress Control Number: 2020951465

Summary: In this partially illustrated early chapter book and the second book in the
Charlie's Rules series, eleven-year-old Charlie and his new best friend, Amy, figure
out why a puppy is attacking its owner and save both her and the dog's lives.

Orca Book Publishers is committed to reducing the consumption of
nonrenewable resources in the making of our books. We make every
effort to use materials that support a sustainable future.

Orca Book Publishers gratefully acknowledges the support for its publishing
programs provided by the following agencies: the Government of Canada,
the Canada Council for the Arts and the Province of British Columbia
through the BC Arts Council and the Book Publishing Tax Credit.

Cover and interior illustrations by Sabrina Gendron
Design by Dahlia Yuen
Edited by Liz Kemp
Author photo by Rebecca Wellman

Printed and bound in Canada.

24   23   22   21 • 1   2   3   4

Charlie's Rules series

Pasture Bedtime

Ruff Day

Chapter One

"You both work for a veterinarian," Jenna said to Charlie and Amy. Jenna's expression was serious. "If a dog keeps attacking someone, do the police take it away and put it to sleep?"

Charlie Dembinski, Amy Ma and Jenna Yee sat in the back of the classroom. All of Mrs. Gibson's students were working in small groups on their science projects.

Jenna's question didn't apply to their research on the solar system.

And normally, when there was work to do, Charlie liked crossing it off his list as soon as possible. However, Charlie realized that Jenna's question might help him now.

Charlie glanced down at his open notebook on the desk, in which he had carefully written four points:

1. <u>Charlie Dembinski</u>: ~~The asteroid belt. How it was formed and does it affect the orbit of Mars.~~
2. <u>Jenna Yee</u>: The oceans of Mars and what happened to them.
3. <u>Amy Ma</u>: The moons of Mars. Description and history of discovery.

Bonus:

4. <u>See if Amy figures this out</u>: Ma is as selfless as I am.
   (Start with something like: Amy loves helping people.)

"Tell me more about this dog that's attacking people," Charlie said to Jenna. He flipped to an empty page in his notebook and held his pencil ready. "It sounds serious. Maybe Amy can help."

He paused, took a deep breath and then said it. "Ma is as selfless as I am."

Charlie waited for Amy to speak. But Amy was busy typing on her laptop, probably trying to finish the work she had promised would be ready for today, Charlie thought.

Amy's rare silence was perfect. Later he would remind her why. Amy and Charlie had only recently become friends. She was new to the school and new to Charlie's life, but Charlie thought he already knew her pretty well. Charlie's mother, Selena, was a veterinarian, and Amy's mom had recently started working as Selena's bookkeeper. This meant that Amy and her mom lived in the guesthouse on Charlie's family's ranch.

"We don't need to report it!" Jenna said quickly. "I only asked what *if*. And I'm only asking for a friend."

"Oh." Charlie crossed number four off his list, ~~Ma is as selfless as I am~~. Finally he had a victory against Amy!

He put his pencil down. "Jenna, I'm glad that was only an *if* question. Because *if* a dog was attacking someone, it would need to stop."

"Yes," Jenna said. "Forget I asked, okay?"

"Sure," Charlie said. He looked at his list. Only two more things to cross off. "How are each of you doing on your reports? Our group presentation is next week."

He was very nervous about the presentation. He would have to stand in front of everyone as they stared at him, and Charlie did not like attention.

Something bumped Charlie's foot. It was their classroom rabbit, Smokey. Mrs. Gibson was a fun teacher. She thought having a rabbit in the classroom would relax students who needed relaxing. Smokey knew how to use a litter box and hopped around where she wanted. There was a gate at the classroom doorway to keep her from going in the hallway. Sometimes Amy was one of the students who relaxed better because of Smokey.

Right now, though, it was Charlie who needed help. He reached down and lifted Smokey into his lap, and right away he started feeling less nervous.

Amy finally stopped clicking on the keyboard. "I don't want to write about the moons of Mars. Check this out. There is some really awesome stuff about space travel."

She grinned as she turned the laptop toward him. Amy grinned a lot.

"We can't switch." Charlie didn't want to look at the screen. "We've already decided what we are doing, as a group. I wrote it down."

Now he was nervous that Amy might change the presentation. He held Smokey closer.

"Charlie probably crossed off his task on the first day," Amy said to Jenna. "I haven't known him for very long, but I already know about all his rules that he likes to follow. By the way,

Charlie. Very clever. Ma is as selfless as I am."

Charlie sighed. Amy had figured it out—too bad.

"Ma is as selfless as I am?" Jenna repeated.

"Like my name. Amy Ma," Amy answered. "Just like *race car*, it reads the same way forward as it does backward. That's called a palindrome. Charlie likes to see if he can say one without me noticing."

Charlie turned the page so that Jenna could read it for herself. *Ma is as selfless as I am.*

"Cool," she said when she figured it out. "Really cool."

But not much of a smile crossed her face.

"About switching my part of the project," Amy said, smiling. "It's never too late to try new things!"

Charlie felt his stomach tighten. He hoped Jenna had at least finished her part already.

"Jenna," Charlie said, "how are you doing?"

"Charlie." Amy spoke in a patient voice. "Weren't you listening? Her dog is attacking someone. She's worried the police might take it from her."

"I meant with her report," Charlie said. "Besides, Jenna said she was asking for a—"

That's when Charlie noticed the tears trickling from Jenna's eyes.

"Charlie," Amy said in a soft voice. "I think Jenna needs Smokey."

Charlie passed Smokey to Jenna. She cuddled the rabbit to her face. "Can we talk about the project later? I am really, *really* worried about my dog, Diesel. He's the best bulldog in the world, but he keeps attacking my mother."

Chapter Two

When the bus dropped Charlie and Amy off at the side of the road after school, Amy ran to the clinic and left Charlie behind at the stop.

As always, Charlie stood still for a moment to enjoy how good it felt to be home. A narrow gravel driveway led from the road to a white ranch house where he lived with his mom and dad and baby sister. Amy and her mom lived in the smaller white guesthouse beside it. Behind the houses were three red barns, and behind that was a long view to faraway hills on the horizon.

Charlie helped his dad with the cattle, and he helped his mom in her veterinary business. One of his weekly tasks was to change the letters on the bottom half of her clinic's sign beside the road. The top half always stayed the same:

DEMBINSKI VETERINARY CLINIC
DR. SELENA DEMBINSKI, DVM
(Open weekends)

DVM stood for Doctor of Veterinary Medicine. Charlie was proud of his mom. It took a lot of work and dedication to become a veterinarian.

Charlie was less proud of the bottom half of the sign. **What do you call it when a cat wins first place at a dog show? A cat-has-trophy!**

Charlie didn't like puns. It was torture to put up a new one each week.

DEMBINSKI VETERINARY CLINIC
DR. SELENA DEMBINSKI, DVM
(Open weekends)
What do you call it when a cat wins
first place at a dog show?
A cat-has-trophy!

Why did Mozart end up getting rid of his chickens? Because they kept saying, "Bach, bach!" But, letter by letter, he always did his job.

He walked down the gravel road and into the waiting room of his mom's clinic. Nobody was there except for Amy. On days when the receptionist had to leave early, he or Amy would sit behind the counter to answer the phone and book appointments on the computer.

Amy wasn't at the computer though. She was sitting in the reception area, holding a huge cat with long brown and black fur. As Charlie walked in, she popped a big bubble of gum she'd been chewing.

"This is Ted," Amy said. "He looks big, but he's really light."

"Make sure owners stay with their pets," Charlie said. "Rule 15."

Charlie always carried a small notebook in his back pocket in which he wrote different rules he had learned while working with animals. Rules like *Pigs never poop when walking, so when they stop, watch out* and *Never get in the way of an owl wearing a blindfold.*

"Unless they have goats that poop," Amy said. "Maybe you should add that to the rule."

The week before, someone had brought a sick goat into the reception area. When it pooped on the floor, the smell made the owner run outside to throw up.

Charlie pulled his notebook out. He added *unless the owner needs to throw up* to rule 15. Rule 52 was *Make sure sick goats stay outside.*

"And maybe you should add something else to rule 15." Amy chomped her gum and pointed down the hall at the closed bathroom door. "Mrs. Tompkins didn't leave. She is doing what the goat did...just not on the floor."

They both heard the toilet flush.

"Oh," Charlie said. "Did you at least make sure all the forms were filled out when she got here?"

"Ted can barely move. It seemed more important that I hold him for Mrs. Tompkins."

She stood and walked toward Charlie. "Give him a hug. You'll see what I mean."

Amy had once saved the life of a dog because she had paid closer attention to how the dog was acting than to what his paperwork said. Charlie reminded himself to be less concerned about rules and more concerned about the animals and people. He really wanted to step away from the cat and check the paperwork, but he took a deep breath and held out his arms. He reminded himself that he kept a lint roller behind the counter, and it wouldn't take too long to remove all the cat hairs from his shirt.

The cat purred against Charlie's chest. That felt nice—maybe it was worth the work of cleaning his shirt later.

"You are correct. Ted hardly weighs anything."

Charlie preferred to use the word *correct* instead of *right*. After all, while *right* could mean correct, it could also refer to the opposite of left. It was important, Charlie felt, to use precise language.

"It feels like he's eaten a big ball," Amy said.

Charlie felt a huge lump in Ted's belly. "That can't be good."

"Cancer. Mrs. Tompkins is new to the area. She said her old vet guessed Ted might only live for a few months. But that was a year ago, and now the tumor is really big. Ted isn't eating. She thinks he's going to die any day now."

"That's sad," Charlie said and handed the cat back to Amy. This was really as long as he could go without following his rules. "You did make sure Mrs. Tompkins filled out all the forms, correct?"

"Maybe...maybe not," Amy said. She blew a bubble with her gum, popped it and grinned.

Charlie knew that meant *not*. He walked to the desk to find the correct forms for Ted. But first the lint roller.

Mrs. Tompkins returned to the waiting area just as Charlie had finished brushing off the last of the cat hair.

She gave Amy a brave smile. "I'll take Ted. You said you needed to go help a friend? I see I am the last one here, and it's nearly closing time."

"Thanks, Mrs. Tompkins," Amy said. "Dr. Dembinski knows you are here. She'll be out right away. Ted is in good hands. No matter what happens."

Mrs. Tompkins gave another brave smile. "I hope so. I really love Ted."

Amy patted Mrs. Tompkins on the shoulder. Then Amy headed to the door and motioned for Charlie to follow. The empty forms bothered him, but Jenna needed their help.

Chapter Three

"It's not my fault that I found out other cool stuff about the Apollo missions that put astronauts on our moon!" Amy said. "And by the way, you didn't notice, but I won. Again. Though I *am* impressed that you never quit trying to beat me."

Even if Charlie had wanted to answer, which he didn't, he couldn't, as he was currently gasping for breath. How Amy managed to talk immediately after a bicycle race amazed him.

If Amy and Charlie wanted to visit friends in town once they were home from school, they rode their bicycles from the ranch, along a road with few cars and lots of trees. Charlie preferred riding quietly and slowly so that he could get lost in mentally planning out upcoming tasks.

But with Amy, the rides were never quiet. Charlie had learned that the best way to keep her from talking nonstop was to challenge her to a race. Amy was very competitive, and when she was racing, she focused solely on winning. Even if she *was* talking, Charlie wouldn't hear her, because he always let her get way ahead so he could pretend he was alone.

"Anyway," she continued, "one thing I learned was that on the Apollo missions, their spaceships were so small that there

were no showers. Or toilets. And you can't spend days and days traveling in space without pooping, right?"

They were pedaling slower now and were almost to Jenna's house. There was a chain-link fence around the yard. They could see Jenna sitting on the steps with a bulldog beside her.

"Look," Charlie said. He didn't want to talk about pooping astronauts. "Jenna is waiting for us."

Jenna waved when she saw them. The bulldog stood, pulling on the leash Jenna was holding.

"Giant sandwich bags," Amy said, waving back at Jenna.

Charlie frowned. Mentally he tried reading "giant sandwich bags" backward. When Amy blurted something that didn't make sense, it was often a palindrome.

Like "murder for a jar of red rum." Or "oozy rat in a sanitary zoo."

This wasn't a palindrome, though, so Charlie had no choice but to ask. "What about giant sandwich bags?"

"They were officially called *fecal bags*," Amy said. "Fecal is a scientific name for poop. Astronauts opened the bags and pooped in them."

"I don't need to hear this." Charlie leaned his bike against the fence and took out his notebook and pencil from the handlebar bag. Taking accurate notes was going to be important if they were going to help Jenna. "By the way, I've known Jenna since kindergarten. Her mom is the only person I know who likes chewing gum more than you do."

"Great! I had to swallow mine to race you here." Amy dropped her bicycle next to Charlie's. "And I don't have any more. Maybe she'll let me a have a piece? As long as it's not too minty. Grown-ups always chew minty gum, and I prefer gum that lets you blow giant bubbles."

Charlie picked up Amy's bike and leaned it against the fence. "It's bad to swallow chewing gum."

"Nope. That's just a myth. Google it. Once you swallow it and it's in you, it goes out like everything else. Even if you poop in outer space."

"Hey, Jenna," Charlie called as she walked toward them, holding her dog on his leash. Maybe Amy would stop talking about poop.

"So how about I switch my part of the report to fecal bags?" Amy continued. "That's *way* more interesting than the moons of Mars."

"We had a plan," Charlie answered. "We—"

"Thanks for coming over," Jenna said, just short of the gate. "I told my mom we were going to work on the project. We will, of course, but I'm so glad you said you would try to help me with Diesel."

"I love your dog!" Amy said as Jenna opened the gate. Diesel was a little bulldog, mainly white with a brown patch on the side of his face.

He pulled hard against his leash, butt wagging, excited to meet Charlie and Amy. Or maybe, Charlie had a quick thought, Diesel wanted to attack them like he'd attacked Jenna's mom?

"Diesel, you are beautiful!" Amy said.

"Is it safe to pet him?" Charlie asked. They were, after all, here because Jenna was worried about Diesel's behavior.

"Very safe," Jenna said. "He's never actually bit anyone. And he only growls at my mom."

Amy dropped to her knees and held out her arms to Diesel.

Charlie wasn't so sure about getting that close. There was some drool on the side of Diesel's mouth. Cat hair you could remove with a lint brush. Bulldog drool, not so much.

Amy didn't seem to care about the drool. She hugged Diesel and scratched his head. Diesel panted, his tongue hanging out and his little tail wagging his whole body.

Jenna smiled. "He's only a year old. We call him Dees for short."

"Um, he seems really friendly," Charlie said, confused.

"He is," Jenna said. "He's the best dog in the world. He's friendly with everyone, except sometimes my mom. If we have to get rid of him, I'll cry and cry forever."

Chapter Four

The three of them walked up the steps with Dees. Jenna opened the front door and took off his leash. Then she walked Charlie and Amy through the living room and into the kitchen.

Mrs. Yee had the oven door open. Her jaw moved slightly as she looked at what was in the oven. Just as Charlie had expected, she was chewing gum. The perfume she wore was strong enough for Charlie to smell, even with cookies baking.

Standing beside her was Lauren, Jenna's younger sister. Lauren was wearing giant oven mitts.

"Smells great, Mom," Jenna said. "You remember Charlie. And this is Amy. She's new to our school."

"Nice to see both of you," Mrs. Yee said. She had a great smile. "Lauren baked these cookies for you."

Lauren reached into the oven to pull out a tray of chocolate chip cookies. She set the tray on top of the oven.

"I make the best cookies ever," Lauren said. She was three grades behind Jenna. "Can I hang out with you? I'll just listen and eat cookies."

Not a good idea, Charlie thought. He and Amy were really there to learn more about why Dees was attacking Mrs. Yee. He had not written this down

in his notebook yet, but it was on his mental list.

"How about next time?" Jenna said. "When we have our presentation ready, you can be our audience when we practice."

"Sure!" Lauren grinned. "Promise?"

"Promise," Jenna said. "And I'll play video games with you tonight after you finish your homework."

"Worst sister ever," Lauren said, grinning. "Just kidding. Best sister ever. I'll head to my room to do my homework."

"You take Dees then, Lauren," Mrs. Yee said. "Amy and Charlie and Jenna, you can take some cookies to the den."

"Do you have any gum?" Amy asked. "I think better when I'm chewing."

"Me too," Mrs. Yee said. "You might not like mine though. It's a minty mouthwash gum that brushes your teeth when you chew. I figure if I'm chewing gum, I should make it good for me."

Amy laughed. "Okay, maybe after the cookies."

Charlie watched Dees closely to see if he would growl and attack Mrs. Yee, but he simply lay beside Jenna until Lauren called for him and they went to her room.

They left Mrs. Yee in the kitchen and got comfortable in the den.

"Everything looked okay with Dees," Amy said, biting into a cookie.

"It doesn't happen all the time," Jenna said. "But when it does, it's scary."

"I know you didn't want to talk about it at school," Amy said. "But we're here to listen. Then we can ask Dr. Dembinski for advice."

Charlie had his notebook and pencil ready.

"Maybe don't write stuff down," Jenna said. "And let's not ask your mom for advice, Charlie. I'm not sure I want any other grown-ups to know about this. In case they take Dees away from us. Maybe you two can figure it out first?"

Charlie gave that some thought.

"Jenna," he finally said. "If it's something we need to keep secret from grown-ups because it's dangerous, it's probably something we should be asking them for help with."

"Don't take that personally," Amy said to her. "Charlie likes to follow rules. Sometimes I don't think that's as important as he does, but in this case, I agree with him. If Dees really does attack people, what if Lauren is next? Or you?

Or a baby? Then all of us would feel bad."

"Mom keeps saying he will grow out of it. Does that help?" Jenna asked.

"You can trust my mom to do everything she can to help Dees," Charlie said. "I think we need to tell her."

Jenna nodded, but she was close to tears again.

"Amy and I googled why dogs might bite people," Charlie said. "Just in case there was stuff we didn't know from working in the clinic. I wrote the reasons down."

He opened his notebook and showed Jenna.

1. Defending itself.
2. Startled.
3. Abused.

4. *Someone is running away and it thinks they are playing.*
5. *It is ill.*

"I googled it too," Jenna said. "But none of those reasons make sense."

"He seemed friendly with your mom in the kitchen," Amy said.

"That's just it," Jenna said. "It's only once in a while. He leans in close to her, then starts to growl and then bark. And then he tries to bite her legs."

"Has he broken through the skin yet?" Charlie asked. He really should be writing down all of this information.

"No," Jenna said. "He just nips at her legs, but each time it gets a little worse, and I have to pull him away."

"Does he try to bite you when you do that?" Amy asked.

"Never. But he pulls hard for me to let him go so he can get to my mom. We end up putting him in another room until he calms down."

"Huh," Amy said. "I'll bet you're worried he might actually bite hard enough to make her bleed."

Jenna nodded. "When I googled it, I also learned you have to report dog bites to the authorities. And that they might euth...euth...euth..."

She wasn't able to finish the word.

"Euthanize it," Charlie said helpfully. "That means—"

"Charlie," Amy said. "Have a cookie."

Amy hugged Jenna. "I understand how you feel. We promise to do what we can. Next time this happens, can you take a video of it for us?"

"Maybe," Jenna said. "But I think I might be too busy pulling Dees off my mom to hold my phone and record. I don't want to ask Lauren to do it because I don't want to explain to her what I'm doing. If they have to take Dees and put him to sleep, it will be the worst thing ever for us."

Jenna was holding back tears. "Maybe we should work on our science project so I don't have to think about this anymore."

"Great idea," Amy said. "Let me tell you about astronauts and poop bags. And why I want to change my part of the report."

Charlie sighed. He did that a lot when Amy was around.

Chapter Five

The following day Charlie and Amy stepped into the veterinary clinic after school. Nobody else was there.

"I'd like to ask your opinion about something," Amy said to Charlie.

"Nice of you to ask," he said. "Usually you just tell me."

"Ha ha. It's about cars," she said.

"Don't know a lot about cars," he said. "But I'll do my best."

"A Toyota. Race fast. Safe car. A Toyota."

Charlie titled his head to think. "Are you asking if I agree?"

She nodded.

He thought some more and realized he had been correct. Amy rarely asked for his opinion. So what was she really asking?

A Toyota. Race fast. Safe car. A Toyota.

"Nice try," he told Amy a few seconds later. "Same forward as backward."

Her face lit up with a grin, and she gave him a high five. "Well done!"

That was one thing he really liked about Amy. She was always happy for other people.

Selena walked into the waiting area. She was wearing her usual lab coat over a gray sweater and jeans. She wore blue rubber gloves and held a white plastic garbage bag. When Charlie and Amy were working for her in the clinic, she preferred to be called Selena. At home Charlie called her Mom. He liked this arrangement. A lot.

"Would you like to see something amazing—and gross?" Selena asked.

"Yes," Amy said.

"No," Charlie said—but he knew he'd look anyway.

Selena lowered her hands so that Amy could open the top of the bag and peek inside.

"Looks like a dead rat!" Amy said.

Charlie squinted and looked for himself. What he saw was about the size of a cantaloupe. "More like a possum."

"It's a hairball," Selena said. "Biggest I've ever seen. I had to show it to you!"

Amy poked at it with her finger. Charlie winced, thinking of germs.

Without acknowledging him, Amy said, "Yes, Charlie, I'll wash my hands with soap right away."

"What kind of cat could make a hairball that size?" Charlie began. "Wait. It came from Mrs. Tompkins's cat! Ted! He was the biggest cat I've ever seen."

Amy said, "Is Charlie right?"

Is Charlie *correct*, Charlie thought. But Selena had taught him a long time ago to keep those thoughts to himself.

Selena nodded. "When she took Ted to her vet in the other town, Mrs. Tompkins had a daughter who needed financial help. So she agreed when the vet said it would be unnecessary to spend money on an ultrasound just to confirm it was cancer. All these months later, though, his stomach was so big that I couldn't believe Ted would still be alive if it were cancer. So we did the ultrasound, and it was just some kind of foreign mass. I opened up Ted on the operating table, and all I saw was hair!"

"Mrs. Tompkins must have been so happy when you told her," Amy said.

"It was a good day," Selena said. "She started crying tears of joy. This is one of the reasons why I went to medical school."

"Have you ever had to put a dog down because it bit someone?" Amy asked. "That wouldn't be a good day, right?"

"It's very difficult," Selena said. She glanced from Amy to Charlie. "It seems like you have a reason for asking."

"After Amy washes her hands," Charlie blurted out. "Otherwise I won't be able to concentrate."

"Oh, right!" Amy washed her hands and returned. She shook water from her hands. "Said I'd wash them. Didn't say I'd dry them!"

Charlie sighed.

Selena smiled, then said, "You know of a dog that bit someone?"

"Not yet," Amy said. "But our friend Jenna is worried he might."

Amy and Charlie took turns explaining the situation.

"Hmm," Selena said. "Without seeing it for myself, I'm thinking that if Dees really did want to bite, he already would have. There must be something else causing the behavior. You say you're working on a science project with Jenna?"

Just the mention of the project made Charlie feel dread in his stomach.

He'd be standing in front of the classroom *way* too soon.

"We have a really cool project," Amy said. "I'm doing my report on fecal bags."

"Actually, we're still discussing that," Charlie said.

"Let me know how that works out for the both of you," Selena said with a small laugh. "In the meantime, what if you go straight to Jenna's house tomorrow after school instead of taking the bus home. Work on your project with her and try to see if there's anything there that triggers Dees to behave the way you've described."

"Any suggestions?" Amy asked.

"Not quite sure," Selena said. "I don't think blood work would help. If it were a health problem, his behavior would be consistent with everyone. Maybe Mrs. Yee does something differently during the times Dees growls at her." Selena gave them a sad smile. "I hope you can figure it out."

Chapter Six

"Here's the thing," Amy said. "When you open up the fecal bag, you peel off strips of paper from the inside of the top of each side of the bag. Under the strips are lines of sticky tape. Can you guess why the astronauts needed sticky tape?"

It was after school the next day. Jenna, Lauren and Charlie were sitting on the couch in the den as Amy stood in front of them to practice her part of the presentation. Dees was asleep on the floor in front of them. Charlie was using his phone to video her so that Amy could review it afterward and see if she needed to make changes in her presentation. They'd already recorded Charlie and Jenna. He didn't want to see the video of himself—he knew it would be horrible.

"Why did they need sticky tape?" Lauren asked. "I HAVE to know!"

Lauren's yell woke Dees, and he sat up, his tongue flopping down the side of his face.

Charlie felt his forehead crinkle—he was frowning. He'd noticed that when Amy spoke, Lauren sat on the edge of the couch, leaning forward with a big grin on her face. Now she was yelling to get the answer from Amy.

Of course, Charlie thought. Who wouldn't be interested in poop? But his asteroid belt was amazing too.

His notebook was open in his lap. He glanced down at the bullet points he had written on the page.

- *there are millions and millions of asteroids between the orbits of Mars and Jupiter*

- *some are the size of pebbles, some are as big as houses or bigger*

- *asteroids have irregular shapes, like potatoes*

- *asteroids are spread apart— spacecraft can move through without hitting them*

- *asteroids get named from suggestions by their discoverers and are also given a number to identify them*

While Charlie had delivered these amazing facts during his practice presentation, complete with illustrations, Lauren had been leaning back, and she had covered her mouth a few times—like she was yawning. And she hadn't asked a single question.

Before Amy could answer Lauren, Mrs. Yee stepped into the den. She was wearing a T-shirt and shorts. Her hair was wet, like she had just stepped out of the shower. Charlie didn't smell perfume this time.

"Have to know what?" Mrs. Yee asked. "Have to know between me and Lauren who is the better cookie baker? I can bake some and prove it's me, if you like." She smiled.

"Not that question!" Lauren said. To Charlie, it seemed like Lauren was always smiling and giggling. Except when it came to asteroids. "We *have* to know why fecal bags have sticky strips on the inside!"

"Fecal?" Mrs. Yee said.

"That's the scientific name for poop," Lauren said with a serious face. "I'll never again tell you I have to poop. Instead I'll tell you that I need to get rid of some fecal stuff."

"Hmm," Mrs. Yee said. "Poop bag? What kind of report is this?"

She was smiling, like she was interested. Asteroids were more important though, Charlie thought.

"When astronauts needed to poop in space," Amy said, "they used something that looked like a giant sandwich bag. There was sticky tape to make sure the edges of the bag were—you know—taped in place on their butts. They didn't want to miss the bag! Otherwise the poop would float in the air because there's no gravity!"

"Gross!" Mrs. Yee said. Smiling again. "Very gross!"

Dees walked toward her. Mrs. Yee knelt down to pet him. He lifted his head and sniffed at Mrs. Yee's mouth, almost like he wanted to kiss her.

Then Dees barked. Very loudly.

"Dees," Mrs. Yee said in a warning tone. She straightened. "No!"

Amy looked at Charlie and nodded. Charlie lifted his phone and began to video. Mrs. Yee didn't notice because Dees had jumped up on his hind legs and had begun to paw at her knees.

He growled and barked and nipped at her leg, just above the knee.

"No, Dees! No!" Mrs. Yee tried to push Dees away. He pushed back, barked louder and jammed his face into her leg.

Jenna jumped from the couch and grabbed the bulldog's collar.

"Dees!" Jenna shouted.

"Dees!" Lauren was crying.

"Dees!" Mrs. Yee shouted.

Jenna managed to pull Dees away, but he kept growling and pulling toward Mrs. Yee.

"That's it," Mrs. Yee said. She took a deep breath. "We've tried training school. We've tried everything. I'm not sure how much longer Dees can live with our family. What if he were to actually bite one of us?"

Chapter Seven

On Saturday morning Charlie leaned against the fence railing with his dad, Finley, and a rancher named Angus McEwan. They were looking out over

a pasture where cattle moved slowly as they grazed. The sun felt pleasant, and there was a light breeze.

Charlie saw a cow stop at a nearby water tank. He waited for what would happen next. Rule 35 in his notebook: *Head down, tail up—watch out for splatter.*

Sure enough, that's exactly what happened. His dad had explained that cows liked getting water into their system to help with the digestive process, and that cows didn't particularly like to have their tails caked with manure. Charlie liked it when his rules made sense.

"Nice way to kill some time," Dad said, lifting his hat and scratching his head before putting it back on. He was a tall man who wore a cowboy hat and cowboy boots with his jeans and sweatshirt. "Never hurts to take a break."

"Not on a day like this," Mr. McEwan answered. He owned some horses, and Selena was in the barn, filing down the hooves of one of them. "I remember Saturdays as a kid. Didn't do much either. Just like Charlie here." He grinned at Charlie. "Enjoy this while you can. Someday you'll have to work for a living."

"Angus, he's on a break from shoveling horse feed in the back barn," Dad said, patting Charlie's shoulder. "The kid works hard. For me and for his mom. Smart kid too. Did I mention that? You should have been there when someone walked into the clinic with a vibrating dog."

"Vibrating dog?" Angus said.

"Tell him, Charlie," his dad said.

"It was a big dog," Charlie said. "A chocolate Lab. The owner said he couldn't call and make an appointment because he had lost his cell phone somewhere on a walk with his dog the day before and he didn't have another phone. He had to come in because the dog would suddenly start running around in circles. I was at the computer, taking notes as he talked, and just like he said, the dog started shaking and running in circles. Then it stopped and was normal again."

"Seriously?" Mr. McEwan said.

Charlie nodded. "The file on the computer showed that he had brought the dog in before. It liked swallowing things. The time before, Mom had had to operate because it was drooling and vomiting. X-rays showed a big bulge in its intestines. She went in and found two socks and a hand towel."

Mr. McEwan gave a belly laugh. For a moment, Charlie felt like Amy must have felt the day before when Lauren was begging for more of the story about fecal bags.

"Go on, Charlie," Mr. McEwan said. "What happened next?"

"The guy asked me what time it was. Said he was expecting an important call right about then and asked if he could use our phone while he was waiting. He wanted to call that person and explain why he couldn't answer his cell phone. Then the dog jumped up again, ran around in more circles and stopped just as suddenly."

"What?" Mr. McEwan said. "You're kidding!"

Charlie loved having Mr. McEwan's full attention. "Then *I* made the dog go in circles!"

"How?" Mr. McEwan asked.

"I looked up the man's cell phone number and dialed it. Sure enough, the dog started spinning. We felt its ribs, and something inside was vibrating."

It took Mr. McEwan a moment, but then he roared with laughter. "The cell phone hadn't been lost. The dog had swallowed it!"

"Yes, sir," Charlie said. "The owner had called the cell phone company to stop outgoing calls, in case it had been stolen, but he wanted to get all his incoming calls so he could at least listen to the voice mail."

"Well," Mr. McEwan said, "that's a story I won't forget for a long time."

Charlie looked at his dad, who gave him a wink.

That's when Charlie understood why his dad had asked him to tell the story.

Chapter Eight

After Mr. McEwan had loaded his horse into the trailer, Charlie finished his chores around the ranch. Then he knocked on the door to the guesthouse.

Amy opened the door. "Hey, Charlie, what's up?"

"Was it a car or a cat I saw?" Charlie asked.

She stood in the doorway, snapping her gum. "You can't tell the difference between a car and a cat? How about

I explain, so you can add it to all those rules in your notebook."

"Or I could just write it down for you and you could read it yourself," Charlie said, a grin stretching across his face. "Then maybe you'd see…"

Her mouth stopped chewing. Charlie enjoyed watching her as she thought about it.

"Was it a car or a cat I saw…" She snapped her gum again and laughed. "Good one, Charlie! You got me. Is that why you're here?"

"I wanted to ask you something about our school project," he said.

"Sure." She pointed at a couple of rocking chairs on the front porch. "Sit."

They sat and looked out at the yard and the road and enjoyed the quiet for a

few moments. But just a few moments—
Amy was never quiet for long. "Yes,
Charles?"

"My part of our group presentation
is boring," Charlie said. He really was
terrified of doing a bad job in front of
the class.

"True, but I didn't want to say it. You're the group leader. Maybe you could talk about how asteroids might crash into Earth and wipe out cities?"

"That's exactly it," he said. "You're good at stories."

"I just don't think about it," Amy said.

"That's because you like doing things without planning. And you know that I—"

"Have to think and think and plan and plan," Amy said with a smile. "Doesn't mean one way or the other is better or worse. We just do things differently. I've seen you build perfect doghouses. And you know mine fall apart pretty fast."

Charlie pulled out his phone and brought up the videos. "Last night I asked my dad to watch both of our presentations from yesterday at Jenna's house. Lauren loved your presentation but nearly fell asleep during mine. I asked if he thought there was a way a person could plan a good presentation. Turns out there is! After he explained it to me, I watched our presentations again and saw how your way works and mine doesn't."

"Huh," Amy said. "I didn't even know I had a *way*."

"You give your information in a story. Dad said a good story starts with a problem that grabs someone's feelings. Funny or sad or scary or even gross. Then you make the problem worse, so they'll keep listening until the problem is solved for them. How astronauts poop in space is a gross problem that makes you curious about the answer.

That's why Lauren was listening. Describing asteroids is just a bunch of facts. No story to make it interesting."

"Huh," Amy said. "Now I know."

"This morning my dad got me to tell a story that way to Mr. McEwan, and he was totally hooked. Now that I know what to do, I need to find a space story that will be as interesting as yours. Thanks, Amy."

If he had a great story to tell, Charlie had decided, he would be much less nervous about doing the presentation.

Amy snapped her gum. "You know you don't need to ask me for permission to try a new report, right?"

Charlie frowned. "Do that again?"

Amy shrugged. "You know you don't need to ask me for permission, right?"

"No," he said. "Your gum."

She chewed and popped again. "My gum?"

"It just made me think of Mrs. Yee. Remember my mom told us to see if there was something different that might trigger an attack from Dees? Was Mrs. Yee chewing gum when she came into the room yesterday afternoon? Could that be something that makes Dees want to attack?"

"Huh. My mouth was very dry after my practice presentation," Amy said. "I was nearly desperate enough to ask Mrs. Yee for some of her minty mouthwash gum. Except she wasn't chewing any, and it looked like she had just stepped out of the shower, so I didn't bother."

"Maybe it wasn't the gum then," Charlie said. "She wasn't wearing perfume either, so he didn't attack her because he hates the perfume. Back to the drawing board. We need to figure this out for Jenna. And Dees."

"Wait, maybe it *is* the gum," Amy said a second later. "He attacked her when she *wasn't* chewing gum. What if chewing gum stops Dees from being triggered?"

"Well, he did sniff her face just before he started growling," Charlie said. "Like he was trying to find out if she had something in her mouth."

"Except why would Dees care if her breath smells minty? Why attack if he doesn't smell the mint?"

"Weird," Charlie said. "Bad breath shouldn't matter to a dog. Dogs have worse breath than humans. Especially the dogs that are…"

Charlie stopped.

"What?"

"Mom says that when a dog is sick inside, like from cancer, its breath is way worse. Even humans can tell something is wrong, and we don't have a great sense of smell."

"Cancer?" Amy's eyes widened. "May I borrow your phone? I want to google something."

She spoke as she tapped out each word. **"What…does…it…mean…if…a… dog…sniffs…human…breath."**

Her eyes widened even more as she read the results.

"Charlie, check this out," she said, turning the screen toward him. "We need to talk to your mom about this as soon as possible!"

Chapter Nine

"Yo, banana boy," Jenna whispered to Charlie, grinning. She, Amy and Charlie stood at the back of the classroom. Charlie was holding his notebook. Dees was sitting beside Jenna, on the end of his leash. "You nervous?"

Mrs. Gibson was about to call them to the front of the class to begin their science presentation. At the last minute they had decided not to do their project on Mars at all.

Charlie tried to whisper, but nothing came out. He *was* nervous. And what was with *banana boy*?

"We have a great presentation," Amy whispered to Charlie. "You'll do great. Also, one other thing—Jenna just got you with a palindrome."

Charlie tilted his head to think. *Yo, banana boy.*

Charlie groaned. How could he have missed it?

Jenna and Amy giggled, which made Charlie giggle. He felt a little less nervous.

Mrs. Gibson called their names, and the class grew quiet. Dees followed them to the front of the room. Smokey followed them too. It was amazing how calm Dees was being. He didn't have any interest in chasing Smokey, but it didn't hurt to have him on a leash.

"*How Dogs Can Save Lives*," Charlie said in a quiet voice, reading from his pages. He coughed and tried it again a little louder. "*How Dogs Can Save Lives*."

The faces of the classmates in front of him were very polite. That meant they were all bored.

"I'd like to change the title of my report," Charlie said to Mrs. Gibson. "May I start over?"

"Of course, Charlie," she said.

Charlie pointed at Dees. "*How a Bulldog Attack Saved the Life of Jenna's Mom*."

The faces changed. Some of his classmates shrank back in their desks, like they were afraid, and some leaned in closer, trying to get a better look at Dees.

Mrs. Gibson said, "Oh my."

Charlie turned to Jenna, who said, "First I want to show you what the attack looked like. We have a video ready to play on the Smart Board."

Jenna moved to the computer and played the video of Dees lunging at Mrs. Yee.

When it had finished, Mrs. Gibson again said, "Oh my."

Amy stepped to the front of the classroom and began her part of the report. "All of you stink."

Their classmates gasped. Amy was definitely beginning with a problem that grabbed the feelings of her audience.

"You can shower all you like," she said, "you can use soap and perfume, but no matter what you do, to a dog you will always stink. Dogs have very, *very* good noses. In fact, if a dog was a shark, it could smell a single drop of sweat in a swimming pool."

Some of the students groaned. Charlie liked seeing how Amy made the information so fun.

"And you are falling apart right now," Amy continued. "You shed fifty million skin flakes every minute. All of you. Millions upon millions of flakes of skin are floating in our air. And this bulldog beside me can smell those flakes. I am surprised he isn't throwing up at how gross that must be."

Now they laughed. Amy continued describing what all the students would smell like to Dees. When she finished with that, she said, "Dogs can smell one hundred thousand times better than a human. And we only have six million olfactory receptors—those are things in our nose that let us smell—but dogs have up to three hundred million!"

She gave a half bow, and their classmates applauded.

Now it was Charlie's turn. He had wanted to read his points from his notebook, but he remembered what his dad said about how much people enjoy a good story, so he decided to pretend he was leaning on a fence rail, telling Angus McEwan about Dees.

"Jenna's mom, Mrs. Yee, likes to chew gum," Charlie started. "It's a mouthwash gum, and it's really minty. Dees never barked at her when she chewed that gum because the mouthwash smell covered up another smell…a very deadly smell."

Charlie paused. Everyone was very quiet. He had just made them curious by using the word *deadly*. This was much better than boring them with facts.

"As you saw in the video, when Mrs. Yee wasn't chewing that gum, Dees would get really upset, because he could smell from her breath that part of her body was not healthy."

This is what Charlie and Amy had discovered on Google. They had read story after story about owners whose dogs had found a way to tell them they were sick.

"Mrs. Yee had a cancerous mole on her leg, just above her knee," Charlie continued. "In the video, you can see that Dees was trying to nip away that cancer because he knew it was threatening her life."

He looked at Jenna. It was her turn to finish the presentation. Jenna had some tears in her eyes, but this time they were happy tears.

"Yes," Jenna said. "Because of Dees, the doctors found the melanoma early and were able to remove it. Dees saved my mom's life!"

"This is amazing!" Mrs. Gibson said, her hand on her chest.

"It *was* amazing," Charlie said to the class. "Doctors can test blood for cancer because there are ways of looking for bad blood cells. Doctors are learning that dogs can smell cancer in blood samples nearly 100 percent of the time. Dogs can also smell those bad blood cells in the air from someone's breath. And even in what comes out of the other end of the body. That's why some dogs are now being trained to detect cancer."

"And Dees is amazing," Jenna said. She crouched on the floor to hug Dees as

tears rolled down her cheeks. The whole class cheered.

Charlie didn't even mind when he realized he was crying too.

Wow, he thought, not a bad presentation at all.

And to make it a perfect day, later, when he found a chance, he'd see if he could get this one past Amy:

Too bad I hid a boot.

Author's Note

I hope you enjoyed this story as much as I enjoyed learning from the true stories behind the situations that Charlie and Amy faced in *Ruff Day*. Everything that Charlie, Amy and Jenna present in their report comes from real-life experiences of owners whose dogs helped them discover they were sick.

If you become a veterinarian someday, who knows what kind of fun stories you'll be able to share about the animals you help. *And* the animals who help you!

Sigmund Brouwer is the award-winning author of over 100 books for young readers, with close to 4 million books in print. He has won the Christy Book of the Year and an Arthur Ellis Award, as well as being nominated for two TD Canadian Children's Literature Awards and the Red Maple Award. He is the author of the Justine McKeen series and the Howling Timberwolves series in the Orca Echoes line. For years, Sigmund has captivated students with his Rock & Roll Literacy Show and Story Ninja program during his school visits, reaching up to 80,000 students per year. Sigmund lives in Red Deer, Alberta.